SENEGAL SLEUTHS

SENEGAL SLEUTHS

Barbara Youree

BEACON HILL PRESS
OF KANSAS CITY

Copyright 2006
by Beacon Hill Press of Kansas City

Printed in the United States of America

ISBN 083-412-226X

Cover Design: Keith Alexander
Illustrator: Phyllis Pollema-Cahill

Editor: Donna Manning
Editorial Assistant: Allison Southerland

Note: This fictional story reflects the challenges missionaries face as they serve in another country and gives insight into the culture of Senegal. It is part of the *Kidz Passport to Missions* curriculum.

10   9   8   7   6   5   4   3   2   1

Contents

1
Blown Away

"Who are those guys over there, talking to Maa-mut [ma-MOOT]?" I whispered to my three friends. We knew Maamut because he helped at the clinic here in Senegal [SEN-uh-gawl], but I'd never seen those other men. They wore close-fitting caps without a brim, called skullcaps. They were dressed in baggy pants and loose, sleeveless garments, called tunics. Of course, Maamut dressed like that too. They all looked about 20 years old—the same age as Maamut.

"They're arguing, Jenny," said Abdu [Ab-doo], as he watched the mysterious strangers.

I guess he didn't know who they were either. Everyone knows everyone else here, especially on this side of the village.

We had just finished a soccer game in an open area outside our missionary complex. Even in my divided skirt, called culottes, and a T-shirt, I was hot and sweaty. The sun hung like a big orange ball over the straw rooftops of the village. It looked more like a big moon through the dust that filled the air.

My friends were still in their dark green school uniforms. Abdu wore a tunic over long pants, and Kumba [KEWM-bah] wore a dress just below her knees. We'd stopped playing soccer because black clouds were rolling toward us. Abdu said a bad dust storm was coming, so we'd better head for home. Abdu is 12, and he knows just about everything.

"Let's scout them out," I said, maybe a bit too loud.

"Shhh, Jenny," said Josh. He motioned for us to hide behind two enormous baobab [BAY-oh-bob] trees grown together. Baobabs have short, fat limbs that look more like roots.

"Yeah, let's spy," said Kumba in her soft voice. She's Abdu's sister and my best friend. She wears her hair in short, tight braids. We're both 11. Josh is 10. His mom teaches in the literacy program, and his dad leads Bible studies.

We slipped behind the baobabs just as a wind whipped red dust around us. It stung my eyes and got in my mouth and nose. But we had to hear what these strangers were telling Maamut. The men stood close to the other side of the fat trees and leaned against them to get out of the wind. They had no idea we were snooping.

"We'll see that you lose your job, you thief!" one of the men snarled.

The men were speaking in Wolof [WOH-luf]. And I know the Wolof language better than any of the other missionary kids. Of course, Abdu and Kumba know the language. They *are* Wolofs.

Josh looked at me with question-mark eyes.

"Thief. He says Maamut's a thief." I translated the words for Josh.

We heard Maamut reply, "Dr. Barnes knows I wouldn't steal one of your cows."

Cows are like money to the Wolofs. They almost never kill them to eat. By the way, Dr. Barnes is my dad, and I know he trusts Maamut.

All of a sudden, the wind flattened us against the tree trunks. It was almost dark as night. This was a big dust storm, all right! I heard only a few more words of the men's conversation.

". . . Christian . . ."

". . . thanks . . . to Allah [AH-lah] . . ."

". . . in our village . . . again . . ."

When I peeked around the trunk, the men were gone. Blown away, I guess.

We peeled ourselves off the trees and tried to walk against the wind. Since we didn't have our masks with us, we put one hand over our nose and mouth and squinted our eyes.

"Don't say anything . . . about . . ." The rest of Abdu's words disappeared with him and his sister Kumba into the dust cloud. I hoped this wind wouldn't smash their mud huts.

Josh and I headed home. Our complex had six houses, a clinic, and a library. Somehow, Josh was still holding on to our soccer ball. When we reached the door to his cement-block house, he nodded good-bye.

I could hear the sound of sand hitting the tin roofs. When I turned the knob of my front door, it banged open and nearly knocked Mom over. Half the storm came in with me. It took both of us to close the door.

"What took you so long, Jenny?" asked Mom.

"Oh, we saw Maamut," I said.

"Maamut didn't come to the clinic today," Dad commented. "Are you all right, Jenny?"

"Yeah, I'm fine. But Dad, you look weird, all covered with red dust. You look like a termite mound." I giggled.

He got up from his chair and dusted himself off.

We had a good laugh. We'd been through lots of dust storms, but we'd never seen one like this before. Everything in the room was covered with that red dust. I could smell it, taste it, and feel the gritty dust on my arms and face and in my teeth.

"I believe this is the worst dust storm we've had in the three years we've been here in Senegal," said Dad.

I went to the bathroom and filled the basin with water. I used a washcloth, but the dust just turned to muddy streaks. My short blond hair felt like dry grass.

As I scrubbed, I wondered if Maamut was a thief and why he didn't come to work today. Who were those strangers? Could they really make him lose his job?

2

Not Worth It

Although the wind stopped after three days, dust still hung in the hot air. Now everyone had to clean up the mess.

Since Kumba's mother works for us, she began scrubbing down everything in our house. Kumba and I worked hard helping her. When I looked out the window and saw Josh coming to our door, I hoped he was bringing us a good excuse to quit. And he did.

I opened the door before he could knock. He said, "Do you want to walk to the store and get some blackberry pop?"

Kumba's mom gave us permission, and we were out of there. Maamut saw us leaving and called to us from the roof of the clinic. He'd come back to work and was dusting off the solar panels. The panels catch the sunshine and turn it into electricity. That allows us to keep medicines cool in a refrigerator.

"I'll go with you," Maamut said. We waited while he climbed down the ladder. He had lots of explaining to do. Kumba looked at me, and I knew she was thinking the same thing. We would ask him a bunch of questions.

We stopped by the library where Mom was teaching some ladies to read in Wolof. I waved to her and pointed to the village. She nodded OK.

On the way, we met Kumba's brother Abdu. He had been to his Muslim school. Muslims follow the religion of Islam. Abdu was carrying a wooden board with verses to memorize written on it.

"Peace to you, Maamut," Abdu said and shook his hand. "And peace to you, Jenny, and peace to you, Sister."

We all said, "Peace to you, Abdu. How are you?"

"I am here. And you?"

"We are here. And how are your mother and father?" we said.

"They are there."

Everyone asked about everyone else by name—even how all the cows and goats were. If they were fine, the answer was always "They are there." That's a long way to say "Hello" in Senegal.

Finally, Maamut asked Abdu to join us. He said he would treat us to pop since he had been paid today.

All five of us sat around a little table in front of the shop under the shade of a tree. We sipped blackberry pop from a bottle with a straw. The drink felt warm and sweet in my mouth.

We talked about the dust storm. The straw roof of Kumba's mother's hut had blown off. Kumba shares her mother's hut, so they both went to stay with her grandparents on the other side of the village. They've rebuilt her hut now. Abdu sleeps in his father's hut, and they were fine. Another family lost several huts.

"The rainy season will start soon," said Kumba. "I'll have to help Mother plant the peanuts." Kumba looked at me.

I knew it was time to ask Maamut some questions.

"I hear a storm like that sometimes frightens the cattle," I said as I looked at Maamut out of the corner of my eye and took a sip from my straw.

"Yes, that can happen," said Maamut.

"I guess a person could find one of those wandering cows," Abdu said boldly.

We liked Maamut and didn't want to think he was a thief, but we wanted to know what had happened.

Maamut finished his blackberry pop, while we sat there in silence. No one wanted to change the subject, since Abdu had come to the point.

"Actually, kids, I need your help," Maamut finally said. He glanced around to be sure no one was listening.

"Sure," said Josh, "anything at all."

"We're your friends," said Abdu.

"You see," began Maamut, "all my age-mates are married and live on the other side of the village."

Age-mates of men and age-mates of women stay together their whole lives in Senegal. It's sort of like a club.

"Go on," said Abdu. "I think we saw you talking to some of them the other day by the twin Baobab trees."

"They believe I stole one of their long-horned cows. I was visiting these friends just a few days before the cow disappeared. They pointed out one cow that had been attacked by a hyena [hie-EE-nuh] nearly a year ago. I told them it looked healthy now, except for the scar."

"Is that the one they think you stole?" I asked. I couldn't wait to find out what he wanted us to do to help.

"Yes, that cow didn't come home the night before the storm. Animals can tell when the weather is going to change. I didn't steal it," said Maamut.

"We believe you," said Kumba. We all nodded.

"Why would they accuse you when you're their age-mate?" asked Abdu. He gathered up our empty bottles and set them inside the window of the shop.

15

"They should have asked you to help them find the cow."

"True. But there is something else. I've been attending the men's Bible studies at the library. I like what I hear about the Christian way of life. But it's hard to change your religion here, because we follow certain ways of doing things."

"So they're angry at you about that?" I said.

"Yes, Jenny. Because I'm listening to ideas that seem strange, they think I'm not a true friend to them anymore. They think such ideas could even make me a thief. Of course, they don't understand. And they want to punish me by making me lose my job at the clinic."

"You're such a help to my dad. He says you want to study to be a male nurse," I said. Before, I was just curious, now I felt sorry for Maamut.

"That's right. Dr. Barnes is teaching me many things."

"How can we help?" Josh asked in English. I translated his words to Wolof for Maamut.

"Whenever you see a herd of cows, look for one with a long scar on the left hind leg. Don't tell anyone but me. If I could find the lost cow, I could prove Christian ideas have not made me a thief."

"Is that why you didn't come to work for two days?" I asked. "You were scared?"

"I was afraid they would come to the clinic and cause trouble. I think they plan to tell Dr. Barnes I stole the cow. If I cannot be trusted, they think he will fire me."

"We'll look for the cow," I said.

"We'll be detectives," said Josh.

"Don't worry," said Abdu. "We'll find the cow for you."

"We're your true friends," said Kumba with a smile.

"Thank you. You are good friends." Maamut shook hands with each of us. "But one more thing. I've decided not to go to the Bible studies anymore. Josh, will you tell your dad since he leads the group? I don't want to lose my lifetime friends and my job."

3

Upside Down

Today was market day! I loved seeing the women in their colorful wraparound dresses, carrying bowls of things on their heads or babies tied on their backs. I came to the market with my parents. Of course, Abdu and Kumba were there too. Mom let me go look at stuff with them.

Kumba was wearing a red dress with yellow flowers and a matching turban wrapped around her head. I had on an ordinary pink-checked, loose-fitting dress, called a shift, and flip-flop sandals. Abdu wore an African shirt without a collar and decorated with designs sewn into the cloth. His father made it on his sewing machine.

The men here sew and bake bread in outdoor ovens. Their wives sell the goods. The women also plant and weed the crops. It seems to me like this is upside down—like the baobab trees. Those trees look like they're planted upside down, with their roots sticking up in the air.

We stopped and talked to Kumba and Abdu's dad who was working at his sewing machine. Then we looked at the rows of decorated pottery, colorful clothes, and bags of rice.

A man selling drums was sitting in front of his booth, beating a tomal [TOH-mawl].

When we walked toward him, he stopped playing. "I make the finest tomals," he said. "And they're not too expensive. Here try it." He handed the drum to Abdu.

Abdu tucked the tomal under his arm. He beat a catchy rhythm on it with the special wooden stick.

"Now you play it," said Abdu, handing it to me.

It was beautiful with little ropes along the side, stretching the skin in place. I held it like it was an egg that might break.

"Go ahead," the man said, "put it under your arm so you can squeeze the ropes tight."

I tapped the skin with the stick. Boom-ta-de-boom! "I love it!" I exclaimed, as I handed the drum back to the man.

"Maybe your dad will get it for you," said Abdu. "Kumba and I share a tomal."

"Most people in Senegal play a musical instrument," said Kumba. "Our dad plays the kora [KOH-ruh], a kind of harp with 24 strings."

"I'll ask him," I said. But I knew I'd have to think of a good reason why I needed it.

Mom had said to meet her and Dad by the well, across from the mosque [MAHSK], a building where Muslims worship. Abdu had gone to say prayers, which Muslims do five times a day. Since women and girls can't go into mosques—something else sort of upside down—Kumba was to wait at the well for Abdu too.

Kumba and I sat down on the edge of the public well. Just then, the men started coming out of the mosque where they had prayed to Allah, the Muslim name for God.

"Aren't those two of Maamut's age-mates?" Kumba whispered. "They're talking to the Muslim leaders."

We both stood up and squinted our eyes to see better in the bright sun.

"I'm sure of it," I said. Then we couldn't believe

what we saw next. Abdu was headed straight toward us when the two men stepped in front of him.

We watched them shake hands and greet each other. One of the men pointed his finger at Abdu. Abdu nodded and then hurried over to us.

"What did they say?" I asked.

"Was it about Maamut?" asked Kumba.

"No," said Abdu, shaking his head and looking scared. "They don't know I know Maamut."

"Then what?" we both asked.

"They know our grandparents, Kumba," said Abdu with a frown.

"So what?" she replied.

"How do they know you?" I asked.

"I don't know, Jenny," said Abdu. "But they know my name. They said our father made a big mistake by becoming a Christian."

"He's been a Christian for at least two years," said Kumba. She thought for a moment. "I would get baptized if Mother did."

"Remember what happened to the man who was baptized?" said Abdu. "The other workers cheated him out of his share of the peanut crop."

"But our father never had any problems," added Kumba.

Just then, a man in a striped tunic walked past us. He was herding five or six cows with a long stick.

I turned around and quickly followed them. I did not want the man to know I was looking for a cow with a scar on its left hind leg.

"Hey, Jenny, your parents are here," called Kumba.

When I turned around and saw what my dad was carrying, I forgot about my detective work.

"That's the tomal I played today!" I exclaimed. "Is it for me?"

"Well, yes," Dad answered with a grin. He handed it to me.

Mom smiled. "We were across the street and heard Abdu playing it. Then we saw you beat on it a few times. We thought you would want to take something from Senegal back home when we go for a visit."

"Take good care of it," said Dad.

"Oh, thank you! Thank you! I will," I said, tucking it under my arm. "And if I learn to play it, I'll play in some of the church services. I think that's a good reason to need a drum."

"I'll teach you," offered Abdu. Then he and his sister hurried off through the crowd.

I walked down the dusty road toward home between Mom and Dad. I tapped the tomal lightly and squeezed it under my arm to make different sounds. That made me feel happy inside.

But I felt sad for Kumba and Abdu. I told my parents what the men said to Abdu about their father making a big mistake.

My dad said, "We'll pray for his protection. It's not easy to be a Christian in some countries of the world."

4

Drumbeats

The day Kumba's week-old baby cousin received his name was awesome. That morning, there must have been about 50 people in the road by Kumba and Abdu's compound. We sat on bamboo mats in a huge circle.

The musicians strummed *koras* and beat *tomals,* like mine.

I came with my parents, but Kumba sat next to me. I didn't see her mom and dad anywhere.

"Only musicians whose ancestors have been musicians can play in a ceremony," Kumba explained.

Some women started singing in high-pitched voices. "I can't understand what they're singing about," I said to Kumba.

"Musicians keep the histories of all the families. The women are singing about the deeds of relatives and ancestors of the new baby boy."

"What's your cousin's name?" I asked.

"Nobody knows yet," Kumba said. "His father will name him after someone in the family to honor that person."

The ceremony began when several leaders came and sat in chairs already set up along the road. The new mother followed them, carrying her baby. The drums softened to a slow beat.

The mother handed her baby to one of the chiefs, and the others splashed water all over him. Then the chief who held the baby took out a razor and shaved his head. A week-old baby doesn't have much hair anyway. The baby fussed a bit, and I didn't blame him.

When the music stopped, everyone got quiet.

"What are . . . ?" I started to ask.

"Shhh," interrupted Kumba.

The father of the child came over and took the baby. He lifted him up, then lowered him and whispered in his ear.

"He's telling the baby his name so he will be the first to hear it," explained Kumba.

Then the father said something to one of the musicians. The musician stepped forward and announced, "The baby has been named Massamba [mah-SAHM-bah], after his uncle, Massamba Dem." The child's mother smiled.

No one clapped, but you could see people nodding their heads and hear them whispering to each other. They seemed to approve.

"Massamba is my favorite uncle's name," Kumba told me.

The musician then started saying the names of all the relatives who had lived before Massamba. It reminded me of all those lists of families in the Old Testament.

Since I didn't know any of those people, I started looking around. Suddenly, I noticed a fire behind the crowd. I poked Kumba with my elbow. "What's going on?"

"That's for roasting the goat, Jenny. Didn't you see them slaughter it just as the name was announced?"

"No," I said, "and I'm glad I didn't."

After a short prayer to Allah, the women brought out the food they'd prepared. I liked the steamed rice with peanut sauce best. But I brought my own spoon.

I don't like to dip my hand into the same bowl with everyone else. A few of the others had spoons too.

After lunch, the celebration began. Some people watched wrestling matches. Others clapped in rhythm to the drums.

Abdu joined us, and we went over to look at Massamba. He was sound asleep in his mother's arms. He was such a tiny baby. I was sure he didn't care about the big fuss everyone made over naming him.

There was a pile of gifts on the ground beside Massamba's mother. My mom brought a white blanket she'd bought in Dakar [duh-KAHR], and my dad gave some money.

Abdu and Kumba said they were going home for a while to rest. They said the party would last past midnight. So I looked around for my parents and spotted Dad in the crowd.

Just as I opened my mouth to say, "Hi, Dad," I saw he was talking to some men. I knew I shouldn't interrupt my dad, but I couldn't help hearing part of their conversation.

"No, I trust Maamut," Dad said. "I will talk to him about your missing cow, but he'll keep his job at the clinic."

Although I couldn't see the men's faces, I knew who they were. I was proud of Dad for defending Maamut, but I wondered what the men would try next.

5

Dakar and Sad News

The rains would be coming soon. It couldn't get any hotter or drier than this. Leaves had dried up on the trees. Some people were almost out of supplies, like rice. Men were burning off the dead vines in the peanut fields, so the women could hoe the ground and plant new crops. Smoke hung in the air. I was tired of smelling it.

But today would be exciting. Mom was driving the SUV to the capital city, Dakar, to get five months of supplies. Josh and I loaded empty containers in the back while Mom packed water bottles and snacks.

When Kumba, Abdu, and their mother, Nejobo [nay-JOH-boh], arrived, we piled into the SUV and left. Nejobo works for my family because the government wants missionaries to hire local people. In other words, people who were born in Senegal. That's nice for us too.

On the way to Dakar, we took turns searching for lions, elephants, and zebras with the binoculars. But we didn't see any. Most of the trees that protected them from game hunters have been cut down. Now it's rare to see a big animal. But there were a few monkeys playing in the bare branches of the trees that were left. And because the tall grasses were burned, we could spy a few hyenas.

Our Wolof friends loved the trip as much as Josh and I. Maamut's troubles seemed far away.

"There's a hippo!" exclaimed Kumba, pointing

toward the shore of the Atlantic Ocean. I had never seen one up close like that.

As we approached the city of Dakar, the road along the shore became crowded. Old buses and trucks were crammed with people. Other people walked, carrying all sorts of bundles. Still others rode bicycles. Mom had to drive slowly to keep from hitting the goats and chickens. Long, narrow fishing boats, painted with designs in bright colors, were docked along the shore.

"Look at that old rusty boat," said Abdu. "It's half-sunk in the water."

"Maybe it has a treasure chest in it," said Josh.

"And those pelicans roosting on the bow are guarding it, I suppose," chuckled Abdu.

We saw all sorts of interesting things in the city. The markets were filled with British, German, and French tourists, along with the people of Senegal, all speaking their own languages.

Many people here in the capital city spoke French and wore the same kind of clothes we wear. But others wrapped themselves in their many-colored robes. Women carried baskets on their heads, without holding them! I don't know how they do that. Kumba says it's not hard.

When our plastic containers were full with canned food, medicines, and other necessary supplies, we headed home. I was tired, but happy.

We were on the road to our village—laughing and talking—when Nejobo shocked Mom and me with some sad news. Abdu and Kumba already knew, but they hadn't said anything. Nejobo hardly ever talks, so when she spoke, we got quiet in the backseat.

"My parents have demanded that the children and I move back with them," she said to my mom.

27

I looked at Kumba and moved my lips. "What?"

Kumba nodded, and I could see tears in her eyes.

"My husband loves us and doesn't want us to leave," Nejobo said. "But my parents still have the right to command me."

"I'm sorry," said my mom. "But I don't understand. Is it because of your husband's faith?"

"Yes," said Nejobo. "To me the Christian words are sweet. I like to listen to the Bible stories. But I cannot change. My father and mother . . ."

She didn't finish her sentence, but I knew why she was afraid. The government lets people choose their religion, but relatives can make it hard to choose a different way of life.

Everyone stayed quiet for a long time. I didn't want to ask Kumba and Abdu any questions in front of the grown-ups. I could tell they were sad, and their mother was upset. And Josh didn't quite understand.

I remembered what the men at the mosque told Abdu. They said his father had made a mistake by becoming a Christian. Those were the same men that accused Maamut of stealing their cow.

6

Rain, Rain, Go Away!

Finally, it rained! At first, there were just sprinkles that puffed up the dust. Then light showers came. We could play and splash through the puddles. This week, the heavy rains came with thunder and lightning. We ran through the house closing all the windows.

This morning, it stopped raining. When the sun came out, the water turned to steam. In our missionary school, the fans blew hot air. We have three teachers and 34 students. Usually, we have lots of fun.

But today, I kept messing up on my math problems. Not just because it was hot. I missed Kumba. I hadn't seen her or Abdu since they went to live with their grandparents. And Kumba's mother no longer worked for us, so I couldn't ask her anything.

After classes, Mom said I could go see if Kumba was working in their peanut field. The field is on this side of the village, where they used to live. Kumba could miss school because girls have to help their mothers. But it's important for boys, like Abdu, to get an education.

"May I take her a rice cake or something?"

"That's a thoughtful idea," said Mom. She gave me a whole bag full of rice cakes—so others could have some too. And a big bottle of water.

I could hear the women singing before I got to the field. Then I saw the backs of about six women bent over, working barefoot. Kumba wasn't there. I stood at the edge of the field, not knowing what to do.

It was hot, and I had to squint my eyes in the bright sun. I couldn't tell which woman was Nejobo, Kumba's mother. I knew the age-mates all worked together on each other's fields.

"Jenny, over here!" Kumba was sitting under a shade tree with the young children and babies. She waved.

I ran over. A girl about six years old was asleep with her head on Kumba's lap.

"So you're baby-sitting," I said. "I brought you something."

"Thanks," Kumba said, as she peeked in the sack.

"They're for everyone."

The kids each grabbed a cake and passed the water bottle around.

"This is my little cousin, Awa [AH-wah]. She's sick." Kumba fanned her with a large piece of bark. "She's hot with a fever."

I saw the little pouches of leather tied around her ankle and arm. "She's been to one of your doctors?" I asked.

"Yeah," said Kumba. "Our grandmother took her yesterday. There's medicine made from plants in this pouch. And in this one, there's a verse from the Koran [kuh-RAN], the Muslim holy book. But she's getting worse."

"You could bring her to the clinic," I said.

"Grandmother doesn't believe in Christian . . . in the clinic," Kumba said. "I'm worried."

The women stopped their work and came over to the shade.

"Hello, Jenny," said Nejobo. "Peace to you." We said all the greetings, and I could tell she was glad to see me.

30

Awa's mother took the girl in her arms. "I've got to take my child home," she said.

"Yes, you must go," all the women agreed.

After Awa and her mother left, the others sat down and finished the rice cakes and water. Their empty bowls from lunch sat in a stack with flies and mosquitoes buzzing about them.

"Mosquitoes cause malaria," I said. "I don't know if that's what's wrong with Awa. My father has been seeing a lot of people with malaria since the rains started."

"But can he help them?" Nejobo asked.

"If people aren't too sick—and they don't wait too long," I replied.

"Let's ask Grandmother to take Awa to the clinic," said Kumba.

"We'll see," said Nejobo.

❋　❋　❋

When I got back to the mission complex, people were waiting in a long line to see the doctors. Some were lying on straw mats in the shade. Maamut was handing out bottles of water. The clinic stayed open longer now. More than a hundred people were coming every day.

I wanted to see if Awa's mother had carried her straight to the clinic. I stood in the shadow of the library and looked for them among the waiting people. They weren't there.

I tried to wave at Maamut, but he wasn't looking my way. Then I saw three men who didn't look like patients. They were standing at the end of the line. I watched them yank Maamut's arm and pull him away from the crowd.

Maamut gave them the last of his water bottles. I

31

couldn't believe it! Why be kind to them? Then they all shook hands and everything seemed to be OK. I was glad of that.

Maamut stood facing them in his white clinic jacket, with his hands on his hips. Suddenly, one man seemed angry and shook his fist in Maamut's face. Another man struck a match and held it up in front of him. Maamut went back into the clinic, and the guys walked off drinking their water.

Big black clouds had rolled up and covered the sun. A loud thunderclap scared me. I ran to my house to help close the windows. I wished the rain would go away—and all the other bad stuff too.

7
Prayers for Awa

On Sundays, all of us at the mission complex wear clothes similar to what some of the local people of Senegal wear. Today I wore a long, blue-flowered dress and a turban to match.

I took off my shoes—like everyone else—and left them at the door of the meeting room. Mom and I sat on the women's side.

Kumba and Abdu used to come with both of their parents. Kumba would sit next to me. I missed her. Several others were missing too. There are only a few whose entire families are Christian. They live in the same compound. But Dad thinks there are a lot of secret believers.

While we sang "What a Friend We Have in Jesus" in Wolof, I noticed Josh across the aisle, looking at me. When he caught my eye, he pointed toward the back.

Maamut had just slipped into the last row on the men's side. We grinned at each other. Of course, I had told Josh about Maamut's age-mates coming to the clinic. Maamut hadn't been to services in a long time. I think it took courage for him to come.

Dad got up and read the scripture: "Blessed are you when people insult you, persecute you and falsely say all kinds of evil against you . . ." (Matthew 5:11).

Wow! That described Maamut, all right! And Kumba's father was getting persecuted too. For the first time, he missed Sunday service.

During prayer time, Dad said, "Please encourage your relatives to bring those who are sick to the clinic when they first have fever. Five people died this week while at the clinic—two were children. We have medicine to cure malaria—if they get the medicine in time."

Then my dad prayed for all the names people had put on a prayer list. I'd been praying for Kumba's cousin. Sure enough, Dad mentioned Awa and prayed that her family would bring her to the clinic. That made me feel better. But I was still sad about lots of things.

✻ ✻ ✻

Monday it rained all morning while I was in school. I prayed for Awa between every math problem and after each paragraph in my American history book. But no one would bring a sick child out in this rain.

After classes, Josh came over to play our favorite indoor game—checkers. Finally, the sun came out, and we opened the windows.

"I win!" said Josh. He'd just jumped my last two kings in one move. I guess I wasn't paying attention, because I usually win.

"So what," I said.

A knock at the door stopped him from bragging. I ran to open it.

There stood Kumba, dripping wet. But she had a big smile on her face. "Hi," she said, greeting us the American way.

"Hi yourself, Kumba! Come in. I'll get a towel." I ran to the closet.

I heard Josh say, "We've missed you. Where's Abdu?"

"He's at his Muslim school," she said, as she took the towel.

I noticed her dress. "You went to school today?"

"Yeah. We couldn't work in this downpour."

"You walked all the way from the other side of the village just to see me?"

"Well, not exactly," she said. "I brought food for Grandmother and Awa."

"Awa's in the hospital? How . . . ? In this rain?"

"Awa's father has a donkey cart. He got an umbrella and brought Awa and our grandmother to the clinic early this morning."

God answered my prayers. "How is she?" I asked.

"We don't know yet. Grandmother said they arrived just as the clinic was opening. Everyone went to the library to get out of the rain. Grandmother said one of the doctors read from the Bible something about trusting in God. The doctor said he gives the medicine, but God does the healing. Grandmother repeated those words and seemed to like what he said."

"That was probably my dad," I said. "He says that a lot. One of the doctors always reads a verse and prays over the patients before opening the clinic."

"We thought Awa was going to die last night," said Kumba. "But she couldn't come here until Grandmother approved."

"How is it living with your grandparents?"

"It's nice to be in a compound with all my cousins. I get to take care of baby Massamba," Kumba said. "But there's more work, and Mother and I have to walk a long way to the fields. Mother is sad all the time, and we both miss my father."

"Is your grandmother staying with Awa in one of the five hospital rooms?" I asked. "Will you bring them food tomorrow?"

"Awa's mother will probably come tomorrow after the field work," said Kumba. "Maamut's still at the clinic. I didn't get to talk to him though."

I told Kumba about his age-mates coming and holding a match in front of his face. She didn't seem to be very interested. I guess she was too worried about her cousin.

"I've got to go," Kumba said. "Please pray for Awa. I don't want her to die."

"Of course," I said.

I watched her slosh down the path through the muddy water toward the village. Kumba was my best friend, and I probably wouldn't see her much anymore. I missed Abdu too. He was the leader of our little group. He'd been teaching me to play the tomal when they moved away.

I went to my room and tapped out a sad song on my drum. I knew I had some more big-time praying to do.

8

Together Again

"Miracles do happen," my dad said when he came in for lunch.

I fixed him a sandwich like mine and poured him a cup of coffee.

"Where's your mom?" Dad asked.

"I guess she's still at the women's Bible studies. What miracle?" I started making Mom a different kind of sandwich. We always eat lunch together.

"Guess what?" Mom said, as she rushed in the front door, her face all lit up. "Nejobo came to the class this morning. They've finished planting the peanuts. But I didn't think she would come back to the literacy class."

"Has she moved back home?" I asked. I hoped so. Then I could see my friends again.

"No," said Mom. "But right after class, she was going into the village to see her husband at his sewing shop."

"What about the miracle, Dad?"

"Oh, yes. Well, we should never be surprised at what God does. Especially when we pray for something," he said. "But I've never seen such a complete and wonderful recovery. It's Awa, Kumba's cousin. From a medical point of view, I really didn't think she could make it. I thought they had waited too long to bring her for medicine."

"Awa's cured?" I was really excited about that.

"Yes. Her grandmother said she slept well last night. When I checked her, she sat up and looked around with bright eyes. She said, 'Where am I? I'm hungry.'"

"Is she going home today?" I asked.

"Maamut is going to drive them home in the truck this afternoon. Her fever's completely gone."

I wanted to ask if I could go along, but I knew Dad wouldn't let me. Besides, the grandmother sounded strict.

✳ ✳ ✳

Maamut didn't get back with the truck until after school was out. He must have stayed quite awhile at Awa's compound. I wondered what her relatives thought about her getting well.

One morning about a week after Awa went home, I thought I heard a knock on the door. It wasn't very loud. I was ready to go to school. Mom opened the door.

There stood Nejobo. "I will come work for you again, if you like," she said.

"Of course, I like," said Mom and threw her arms around Nejobo for a big hug.

I wanted to stay and hear why Nejobo was back, but I went to school. When I returned home, Kumba was there too, hanging clothes on the line. She was wearing culottes and a T-shirt like me. I knew she hadn't gone to school.

"Kumba, what are you doing here?"

"We've moved back home!"

I could see tears in her eyes. She rubbed them out with her fist.

"How did that happen?" I asked. "Tell me all about it."

We worked together, hanging up the clothes while she told me.

39

"Of course, everyone in my grandparents' compound was happy about Awa. We had a big meal together to celebrate. Two older people had died of the malaria, and a few others were making a slow recovery. But Awa had gotten well very quickly after going to the clinic."

"We prayed for her," I said.

"I know. We did too."

"You still haven't said why you've come back."

"At the end of our celebration, Mother asked Grandmother if it would be all right to go home. She frowned and said she'd have to ask Grandfather. She said she would tell us the next morning."

"And she did?"

"Yes," said Kumba. "My grandparents said the Christians at the clinic couldn't be too bad since they cured Awa. They said Mother could come back to work here, and we could go back to live in Father's compound. That's why I didn't go to school today. We moved our stuff back to our hut with the new grass roof."

I remembered their roof had blown off in the big dust storm. Now I was getting tired of the rain, and bugs, and mosquitoes. Between the wet and the dry seasons, we would have some nice weather. And lots of fresh fruit, like pineapples and mangoes. Those would be good days.

Just as we finished hanging the clothes, Abdu and Maamut walked into the yard. We ran over to see them. As I passed Kumba's mother, I said, "I'm glad you're back." She just smiled, but I knew she was glad too.

Josh came over and joined us on the thick new grass under a shade tree.

"I guess you still haven't seen a cow with a long scar on the left hind leg," Maamut said.

"I look whenever I see some cows," I said. "But I haven't found her."

"Well, thanks, anyway," he said and turned to Kumba and Abdu. "I talked to your grandparents a long time when I took Awa to your compound. I told them the doctors at the clinic were here to help people. Your grandmother said they took good care of Awa."

"We've moved back here," said Abdu. "And they said Mother could come back to work."

"That gives me courage," said Maamut. "I went back to church last Sunday, and I've decided to return to the Bible studies."

"Are your age-mates still angry at you?" I asked.

"Yes, Jenny. But I believe God is more powerful than they are."

Almost everything was working out fine, except finding the lost cow. It felt good for all of us to be together again.

9

Snoops Hear the Scoop

Abdu and Kumba came over nearly every afternoon now. Since the soccer field was almost dry, Josh and Abdu were kicking the ball around. Kumba and I decided it was too hot to play.

"Let's climb the baobab trees," Kumba said. We did. The new leaves were just sprouting out, so we could sit up there and not be seen by anyone. We sang songs and told jokes. Then we both got quiet and just rested. I could have gone to sleep, sitting on that limb and leaning against the trunk.

Suddenly, I heard voices. I kicked at Kumba's foot that was dangling close to mine. I pointed down below. We listened.

"Day after tomorrow."

"At night. It's got to be after dark."

Maamut's age-mates—four of them this time—were up to no good.

"I know how to get gasoline from a truck."

"Great! I'll bring the torches, and you bring the gasoline."

"We'll break the windows . . ."

"Won't they hear us?"

"Only the guard, if we come after midnight. We'll just hit the glass with a club and throw the lighted torches in. By the time the watchman gets to the clinic, we'll be gone."

"And the fire will be blazing!"

Kumba and I sat still as stones. My hands were sweaty, and I could hardly hold onto the tree.

Then they all shook hands and walked on down the road.

"Day after tomorrow," I said.

"That's just mean," said Kumba.

As we slowly climbed down, we saw Josh and Abdu coming.

"Did you see those guys?" I asked.

"No. What guys?" questioned Josh.

Kumba and I told the boys everything we had heard, word for word.

"Wow! You're good at finding out the facts," said Josh. "That makes you good detectives, or sleuths [SLOOTHS]."

"We've got to tell your father immediately," said Abdu. "This is a serious plot."

We hurried home and found Dad working on a sermon. Abdu told him the whole story. It sounded even scarier when I heard Abdu tell about the plot. I had to correct him a time or two. For example, Abdu thought they wanted to burn down all of our buildings, not just the clinic.

"I'll talk to Maamut first thing in the morning," said Dad. "After the clinic closes, I think both of us should go over to his age-mates' compound."

"I don't want you to get hurt, Dr. Barnes," said Abdu.

"Don't worry," Dad said, "God will be with us. I'll tell them I know about their plot. But I won't say how I know."

"They must be the same guys that talked to me at the mosque," Abdu said. "They told me my father made a mistake by becoming a Christian. I don't know them, but they know me. I think they know my grandparents too."

"They may have had something to do with making you leave your father's compound," added Dad.

"That's what I think," agreed Abdu. "And they probably know about Awa's miracle too."

"That's good. I'll remind them of your cousin's cure at the clinic. We've also helped others from their part of the village."

Josh looked worried. "They said day after tomorrow. There's not much time."

* * *

The next morning, Dad and Maamut left early in the SUV. I didn't think those mean age-mates would pay much attention to them. But I prayed.

School was out now for the summer. Josh and I pitched horseshoes in our front yard until Abdu and Kumba came over.

"We've heard there's a giant termite mound down the road," said Abdu.

"How giant?" asked Josh.

"Twelve feet high!" said Kumba. "They say it's the biggest anyone's ever seen."

"Well, let's check it out," I said.

We told Nejobo, who was working in our kitchen, where we were headed. "Don't go far," she said. "It looks like rain."

Clouds hid the sun, but it was still hot and humid on the dirt road.

"How do the termites build such big hills?" I asked Abdu.

"I don't know exactly," he said. "They dig underground tunnels too. They're blind, and they chew up

dead wood and grass. I think they spit that out to make the mounds."

"That's gross!" exclaimed Josh.

"How much farther is it?" I asked. I remembered Nejobo said it might rain.

"We go off the road a bit, just past that clump of thornbushes up ahead," Abdu said.

As I looked that way, I saw a man coming toward us herding a few cows. I had seen that striped tunic before. He was the man I saw go past the mosque with his cows.

When we reached the man, he stopped. "Peace to you, children," he said. "How are you, Abdu and Kumba?" I guessed they knew each other.

"We are here," said Abdu. "These are our friends, Jenny and Josh from the mission."

"And how are you, Jenny?"

"I am here," I said in Wolof.

"And how are you, Josh?"

Josh didn't say anything, but he shook the man's hand.

"How is your wife?" asked Abdu.

"She is there."

"And your cows?"

"They are here," he said.

Without being too obvious, I looked around at all the cows' left hind legs for a long scar.

When everyone finished the long greeting, Abdu said, "I'm curious. Could you tell me where you got this cow with the scarred leg?" He had spotted it.

The man laughed. "I didn't get her, she just came to me. Last March after that big dust storm, she showed up among my cows. I've tried to find the owner. I don't want to keep a cow that belongs to someone else. Do you know anyone who is missing a cow?"

"We know someone who is accused of stealing a cow like that," said Abdu. "The cow's owner is angry at him."

"Well, Abdu, you know my name and where I live," the man said. "She'll be tied to a stake at my compound every evening with the others. Tell him to come by, and he can have her. Right now I'm looking for grass so they can graze."

"Very well," said Abdu and shook his hand.

The man went on down the road with his cows, and we walked on toward the thornbushes.

"I hope it's not too late to tell Maamut we solved the mystery of the missing cow," I said. "He and my dad are probably talking to those age-mates right now."

"And tomorrow they plan to burn down the clinic," said Kumba.

"When Dr. Barnes tells them he knows about the plot, they may do something worse," said Josh.

"We'll tell Maamut just as soon as they get back," I said.

"There's the giant termite mound," announced Abdu, as he pointed down a narrow path beyond the thornbushes.

It wasn't too far off the road. I couldn't believe it! The mound of red dirt was more than twice as tall as my dad! Some termites fluttered around our heads. "Wow!" I said. "Let's go closer."

Just then, big drops of rain hit our faces, and we turned and ran. Then it started raining hard. We could only walk. The warm rain smelled good and cooled us off. It was fun to splash through the puddles. But after a while, there was so much water, we could hardly see, or even breathe. It seemed to take twice as long to get back.

When we reached home, there sat Dad's SUV. The tires were caked in mud. Mother met us at the door with towels. I could hardly wait to hear what Dad had said to Maamut's age-mates. And we had big news about finding the lost—not stolen—cow!

10
Sometime, Maybe

We were really soaked! I grabbed a towel and hurried to my room. I dried and changed clothes. Josh ran home to change, and then he came back. Kumba and Abdu just dried off, then sat on their towels on kitchen chairs. In just a few minutes we were gathered around the kitchen table.

Maamut and Dad looked serious. I thought the meeting probably didn't go well. Mom brought us lemonade.

"Well, kids," said my Dad, "we didn't talk to the men."

"What happened?" I asked.

"The SUV bogged down in the mud," explained Dad.

"Twice," added Maamut. "Then the rains started. I knew there was a stream up ahead, and that we couldn't cross it with all this rain."

"So we turned around and came back," said Dad. "We'll try again in the morning. This time we'll take the pickup truck."

"And I know another way to go. It's longer, but shouldn't be as muddy," said Maamut.

"But they're coming to set the fire tomorrow night," said Kumba.

"Once they hear we know about their plot," said Maamut, "they won't come. They know you have a guard. We want to convince them that what they're doing is wrong. The clinic has brought help to the people of this village."

"Remember, God blesses those who are persecuted for believing in Him," Dad said.

"And are falsely accused," said Maamut. He remembered Dad's sermon.

"We have something to tell you about that being 'falsely accused' part," I said.

"We found the cow they said you stole." Kumba twisted one of her short braids and grinned.

"What? You found the cow? The one with the long scar on its left hind leg?" said Maamut, excitedly.

"That very one," said Kumba.

"We saw it with our own eyes," said Abdu. "And the man who has it wants to give it back." Abdu told the whole story about meeting the man on the road with the herd of cows. "So you can tell your age-mates, the cow was lost, not stolen."

* * *

The rain didn't stop all night. Usually, I like to hear it hitting the tin roof, but not this time. I couldn't sleep. What if they came tonight instead of tomorrow night? Then I decided they couldn't start a fire in this downpour. So I went to sleep.

When I woke up, the rain had stopped, and the sun was shining in my window.

"Have Dad and Maamut already left?" I asked Mom at breakfast.

She put a piece of buttered toast next to my fried egg and sat down across from me. She poured herself a cup of coffee. "Jenny," she said in her serious voice.

Something was wrong, for sure.

"Your dad couldn't take the time off to go talk to those men. There were too many sick people lined up at the clinic this morning. And we have only three doctors and four nurses."

"But what if they burn down the clinic?" I said with my mouth full. Mom didn't even notice.

"They won't do that, Jenny." She smiled and patted my hand. "You kids did a good job telling your dad about the plot. And finding that cow!"

"What about Maamut?"

Just then I saw Abdu and Kumba coming to the house. I ran to open the door.

"Dr. Barnes is working at the clinic," said Abdu.

"I know," I said.

"Isn't he going to go talk those age-mates out of burning down the clinic?" asked Kumba.

Then they both saw Mom. "Peace to you, Mrs. Barnes. How are you?"

"I am here," she said in Wolof. When they finished the greeting, Mom said, "I was just going to tell Jenny that Maamut left early this morning. He's going to see the man who has the cow. His house is on the way. If all goes well, he will arrive at his age-mates' compound this afternoon."

"He's walking all that way?" I said.

"Won't that be dangerous to go alone?" said Abdu.

"God will be with him," Mom said.

"Of course," said Abdu.

"He and Dr. Barnes talked about what he might say to convince them," said Mom. "And now he will actually have the cow with him—instead of just telling them about it."

* * *

It was hard to wait. Today seemed like a very long day. Maamut might not be back until late at night. Kumba had to help her mother pull weeds in the peanut field. Abdu had to learn verses from the

51

Koran and then go to school. After beating out the three tunes I'd learned on my tomal, I climbed up in the baobab trees with a book. I prayed for Maamut.

Later when we'd finished dinner, Josh came over to play checkers. I won all but one game.

When the clinic closed, Dad left in the truck. He hoped to meet Maamut on the way. Dad hired two extra guards for the clinic—just in case there was trouble.

We waited and waited. Nejobo and Kumba came over and then Abdu joined us. Mom prayed aloud that all would go well. She prayed God would give Maamut the right words to say to his age-mates.

Finally, just as it was getting dark, we heard Dad's truck pull up by the house. Mom opened the door, and we all ran out to meet him and Maamut.

Back inside, we pulled up chairs around the kitchen table. I knew we were safe when I saw the big smile on Maamut's face. Everyone got quiet.

"God has a way of working things out," said Dad. "It seemed like everything was against us yesterday when we couldn't carry out our plan in the rain. But God had a better plan."

"With God's help and the help of Jenny, Abdu, Josh, and Kumba, I could go to my age-mates with the cow," said Maamut.

"You kids are good Senegal sleuths," said Dad.

I grinned with pride, and we all said, "Thanks." Then I turned to Maamut for the rest of the story. "Did they believe you didn't steal the cow?"

"Not at first. They thought I had just been hiding it. When I told them I knew about the plot, they said I brought the cow back because I was scared."

"How did you make them believe you?" asked Abdu.

"Well, first of all, I had a good visit with the man who found the cow. Before handing her over, he put a large sack of rice across the cow's back. He said that was rent for the cow.

"And he wrote a note for me to give the owners. It went something like this: 'This fine young man did not steal your cow. She has been with me since the big dust storm. I'm glad to find the owners. You can thank him for bringing her back to you.'"

"Are your age-mates going to stop bothering you?" I asked.

"Yes. But that's not all," said Maamut. "I think God put words in my mouth. I started talking about how God loves everyone. I told them He is a forgiving God. I don't remember everything I said. Then God gave me the courage to ask them to come to Bible studies with me."

"What did they say?" asked Kumba.

"They said, 'Sometime, maybe.'"

That sounded like a miracle to me.

Kumba squeezed her mother's hand and looked up at her.

Then I heard Nejobo whisper to her in Wolof, "Sometime, maybe, we'll be baptized like your father."